Dear Parents and Educators,

Welcome to Penguin Young Readers! As parents and educators, you know that each child develops at his or her own pace—in terms of speech, critical thinking, and, of course, reading. Penguin Young Readers recognizes this fact. As a result, each Penguin Young Readers book is assigned a traditional easy-to-read level (1–4) as well as a Guided Reading Level (A–P). Both of these systems will help you choose the right book for your child. Please refer to the back of each book for specific leveling information. Penguin Young Readers features esteemed authors and illustrators, stories about favorite characters, fascinating nonfiction, and more!

Young Cam Jansen and the Substitute Mystery

LEVEL **3**

GUIDED READING LEVEL **J**

This book is perfect for a **Transitional Reader** who:
• can read multisyllable and compound words;
• can read words with prefixes and suffixes;
• is able to identify story elements (beginning, middle, end, plot, setting, characters, problem, solution); and
• can understand different points of view.

Here are some **activities** you can do during and after reading this book:
• Character Traits: When Ms. Dee is absent, Mr. Baker is the substitute teacher for Cam's class. On a separate sheet of paper, write down a list of words to describe Mr. Baker.
• Comprehension: Answer the following questions about the story.
  • How did Danny finish his math problems so quickly?
  • Who is Mr. Day?
  • Why won't "clicking" help Cam solve the mystery of the missing coat?
  • What noise do you think Cam heard that helped her solve the mystery?
  • Where does the class finally find Mr. Baker's coat?

Remember, sharing the love of reading with a child is the best gift you can give!

—Bonnie Bader, EdM
  Penguin Young Readers program

*Penguin Young Readers are leveled by independent reviewers applying the standards developed by Irene Fountas and Gay Su Pinnell in *Matching Books to Readers: Using Leveled Books in Guided Reading*, Heinemann, 1999.

To Mom and Dad Hamada—DA

To Diana, Greg, and Hannah Rose—SN

Penguin Young Readers
Published by the Penguin Group
Penguin Group (USA) Inc., 375 Hudson Street, New York, New York 10014, USA
Penguin Group (Canada), 90 Eglinton Avenue East, Suite 700, Toronto, Ontario M4P 2Y3, Canada
(a division of Pearson Penguin Canada Inc.)
Penguin Books Ltd., 80 Strand, London WC2R 0RL, England
Penguin Group Ireland, 25 St. Stephen's Green, Dublin 2, Ireland (a division of Penguin Books Ltd.)
Penguin Group (Australia), 250 Camberwell Road, Camberwell, Victoria 3124, Australia
(a division of Pearson Australia Group Pty. Ltd.)
Penguin Books India Pvt. Ltd., 11 Community Centre, Panchsheel Park, New Delhi—110 017, India
Penguin Group (NZ), 67 Apollo Drive, Rosedale, Auckland 0632, New Zealand
(a division of Pearson New Zealand Ltd.)
Penguin Books (South Africa) (Pty.) Ltd., 24 Sturdee Avenue,
Rosebank, Johannesburg 2196, South Africa

Penguin Books Ltd., Registered Offices: 80 Strand, London WC2R 0RL, England

Text copyright © 2005 by David A. Adler. Illustrations copyright © 2005 by Susanna Natti. All rights reserved. First published in 2005 by Viking and in 2006 by Puffin Books, imprints of Penguin Group (USA) Inc. Published in 2012 by Penguin Young Readers, an imprint of Penguin Group (USA) Inc., 345 Hudson Street, New York, New York 10014. Manufactured in China.

The Library of Congress has cataloged the Viking edition under the following Control Number:
2004017391

ISBN 978-0-14-240660-1   10 9 8

Young Cam Jansen
and the Substitute Mystery

by David A. Adler
illustrated by Susanna Natti

Penguin Young Readers
An Imprint of Penguin Group (USA) Inc.

Contents

Chapter 1
Cam's Amazing Memory

Ms. Dee is out today

"Sit down!" Danny called out.

He was standing on Ms. Dee's desk.

"Ms. Dee is absent, so I'm the

teacher today."

Cam Jansen, her friend Eric Shelton,

and the others in Cam's class did not

sit down.

"Fine, then you're being punished,"

Danny said.

"I won't give you homework!"

A man stood by the door.

He had books and a lunch bag.

"I thought I was the teacher."

Danny jumped off the desk.

He hurried to his seat.

The others in the class hurried

to their seats, too.

"Is this Ms. Dee's class?" the man

asked.

"Yes," Eric said.

The man walked in.

He dropped the books and lunch

bag on Ms. Dee's desk.

"I'm Mr. Baker," he told the class.

"I'm not a baker who bakes.

I'm a Baker who teaches.

Ms. Dee is absent,

so today I'm your teacher."

Mr. Baker sat in Ms. Dee's seat.

"Oh my," he said.

"Ms. Dee left me a note, but

I can't find it."

"There's a paper in your pocket.

Maybe it's the note," said Tim.

Mr. Baker looked in his pants pockets

but didn't find the note.

"It's in your shirt pocket," Tim said.

"Oh, here it is," Mr. Baker said.

He opened the note and read it aloud.

"'I left math work for the class.

It's on the board.'"

Mr. Baker turned to the board.

There was no math work.

"The custodian must have washed it," Eric said.

"Now what do I do?" Mr. Baker asked.

"We all saw it. Ms. Dee wrote it yesterday afternoon, during silent reading," Eric said.

"Now you ask Cam to say, 'Click!'"

"'Click'? What's 'click'?" Mr. Baker asked.

"Cam has an amazing memory," Eric said.

"She has a mental camera with pictures in her head of everything she's seen.

When she wants to remember something, she just says, 'Click!' That's the sound her mental camera makes."

Cam closed her eyes and said, "Click!"

She looked at her mental picture. Then she wrote all the math problems

Ms. Dee had written on the board.
Cam's real name is Jennifer, but
when people found out about her
great memory they called her
"the Camera."

Soon "the Camera" became just
"Cam."

Mr. Baker looked at what Cam had
written.

"You really do have an amazing
memory," he said.

Chapter 2
The Square Egg

Cam's class copied the work from the board.

Danny didn't.

"What do I do next?" Danny asked.

"Next?" Mr. Baker asked.

"Have you done all the math work?"

"No," Danny answered.

"I just want to know if there's something fun to do next."

"You may read a book when you're done," Mr. Baker said.

"I'll read a joke book," Danny said.

Danny quickly copied the math problems.

"I'm done!" he said.

Eric turned and asked, "You have answers to all the problems?"

"Sure, I have answers," Danny said.

"I just wrote any number.

I don't care.

Mr. Baker isn't our real teacher."

"Well, I care," Eric said.

"I want the right answers."

Danny opened his joke book.

"Hey," he asked Eric, "what did the
hen say when she laid a square egg?"

"Sh!" Eric said.

"I'm trying to do my math problems."

"No," Danny told Eric.

"Why would a hen want to
do math problems?
The hen said, 'Ouch!'
That's what the hen said."

"That's very interesting," Eric said.

The children worked on their math problems.

Then they read.

Ring! Ring!

It was the class telephone.

Mr. Baker picked it up.

"Hello," he said and listened.

He put the telephone down and told the class, "That was Dr. Prell, the principal.

She said it's almost time for lunch.

We should take our coats.

After lunch, we'll play outside."

"Yeah!" the children shouted.

"I'm going, too," Mr. Baker said.

Then he looked at his chair.

"There's my lunch, but where's my coat?"

Chapter 3
Cam Solves Mysteries

"Are you sure you wore a coat?"

Eric asked.

"Did I?" Mr. Baker asked himself.

"I drove here this morning.

Look, there's my car."

He pointed to a red car in the

school parking lot.

He checked his pockets.

"Look," he said.

He took everything from his pockets
and put it on Ms. Dee's desk.

"I have papers, bubble gum, pens,
coins, and a wallet," he said.

"My car keys and cell phone
are not here.

I must have left them in my
coat pockets."

Cam said, "Maybe you left
your coat in your car."

"Maybe I did!" Mr. Baker said.

He hurried to the telephone.

He called Dr. Prell.

He asked her to send someone
to watch the class.

A few minutes later Mr. Day, the
gym teacher, walked into the room.

"I'm sorry," Mr. Baker told Mr. Day.

"I forgot where I left my coat.

I'll be right back," he told the class.

Cam watched through the window.

She saw Mr. Baker try to open

the door of his car, but the doors

were locked.

Mr. Baker looked through the

car windows.

Then he walked back inside.

"My coat is not in my car," he said.

"Now what do I do?"

"Now you ask Cam to help you,"

Mr. Day said.

Cam closed her eyes and said, "Click!"
She said, "Click!" again.

"This time clicking won't help," Cam
said, opening her eyes.

"I never saw Mr. Baker's coat."

"I'd like to stay and help," Mr. Day
said, "but I must get back to the gym."

Mr. Baker thanked Mr. Day and sat by
Ms. Dee's desk.

"Now what do I do?" he asked.

Chapter 4
I Need My Coat

"I need my coat," Mr. Baker said.

"It's cold outside.

I need my keys, too."

"Maybe I can help," Eric said.

"We know you wore your coat

to school.

You didn't bring it to class.

So you must have left it somewhere

between your car and this room."

"Where did you go," Cam asked,

"after you left your car?"

Mr. Baker went to the window.

He pointed to the path

by the side of the school.

"I walked there," he said.

"I came into school and

went to the main office."

"That's it!" Eric said.

"You left your coat

in the main office."

Mr. Baker called the main office.

He spoke with Dr. Prell.

Then he shook his head and told

the class, "That's not it.

I didn't leave my coat

in the main office."

"You left the coat on your way
to this room," Eric said.

"Now we walk slowly to the main
office, and look for it."

"That's a good idea," Mr. Baker said.

He stood and said, "Get your coats
and lunches, then follow me."

Mr. Baker took his lunch bag.

The class got their coats and lunches
and followed Mr. Baker.

They looked, and didn't find

Mr. Baker's coat.

"Where's Cam?" Eric asked.

"First I lost my coat," Mr. Baker said.

"Now I lost one of the children."

"You didn't lose her," Danny said.

"She's standing over there with
her eyes closed."

Just then Cam clapped her hands.

"I just remembered something,"
Cam said.

"I know how to find Mr. Baker's coat."

Chapter 5
A Great Idea

"Did you click and remember
something you saw?" Eric asked.

"No," Cam said.

"I remembered something I heard."
Then Cam asked Mr. Baker,

"Did you say you have your keys
and your cell phone in the pockets
of your coat?"

"Yes," Mr. Baker answered.

"Let's call your cell phone.

If it's somewhere between here
and our classroom,
we'll hear the ringing."
"That's a great idea,"
Mr. Baker said.
"I'll use the office telephone."
Cam told her classmates
to spread out in the hall
and listen for the ringing.
Mr. Baker went to the office.
He called his cell phone.

Ring! Ring!

"I hear it! I hear it!" Danny said.

Mr. Baker came out of the office.

"It came from in there," Danny said.

He pointed to the door of the

teachers' room.

Mr. Baker hurried to the teachers'

room.

Cam and the other children did, too.

Mr. Baker opened the door.

There was a green coat on the couch.

"I forgot," Mr. Baker said.

"I came here this morning before
I went to class."

"I'm the one who found your coat,"
Danny said.

"Thank you," Mr. Baker said
to Danny.

"Thank you, too," he said to Cam.

"You remember things you see and hear.

You are amazing."

Mr. Baker opened his lunch bag.

"I prepared my lunch and I forgot what it is!

Oh, I wish I had a *Click! Click!* memory."

He looked in his lunch bag and said, "I wish I had a dessert, too."

The children in Ms. Dee's class ate lunch and shared their desserts with Mr. Baker.

Then they went outside to play.

A Cam Jansen Memory Game

Take another look at the picture on page 31.
Study it.
Blink your eyes and say, "Click!"
Then turn back to this page
and answer these questions:

1. What color is Cam's jacket?

2. Who is on the jungle gym?

3. Where is Mr. Baker?

4. Is there a seesaw in the
   playground?

5. How many people are on the
   swings?